GARDEN OF THE GOOD FOLK AT CHRISTMAS

by **Evelyn Foster**

Published by Country Books
an imprint of Spiral Publishing Ltd

Country Books, 38 Pulla Hill Drive
Storrington, West Sussex RH20 3LS

Tel: 07889 234 964
email: jonathan@spiralpublishing.com

www.spiral-books.com

ISBN 978-1-7395303-4-1

© 2024 Evelyn Foster

The rights of Evelyn Foster for this edition have been asserted in
accordance with the Copyright, Designs and Patents Act 1993.

All rights reserved. No part of this publication may be reproduced, stored
in a retrieval system, or transmitted, in any way or form, or by any means,
electronic, mechanical, photocopying, or otherwise, without the prior
permission of the author and publisher.

British Library Cataloguing in Publication Data.
A catalogue record for this book is available from the
British Library.

Printed and bound in England by 4edge Limited,
22 Eldon Way Industrial Estate, Hockley, Essex SS5 4AD

*For Nicky Mandall:
best of friends
& Helen Smeeton:
best of teachers*

~ Evelyn Foster ~

The illustrations throughout this book are by Charles Robinson (1870~1937)

~ Garden of the Good Folk at Christmas ~

~ CHAPTER ONE ~

THE SECRET MESSAGE

Elfrida Green had a secret. She was half human, half elf! She was a friend to Bright Court Elves (those elves who live in the elven courts) and a rescuer of fairy princesses. Only months ago, she had helped a Bright Court Elf get back to her home in Elfland.

All this, of course, was unusual, but Elfrida was unusual.

She was small and delicate with a pointed nose and slanting green eyes. She loved dressing up both as an elf and as an Edwardian girl. Best of all she had a Magical Garden where elven messages were left for her. This was because Elfrida was friends with Elwin: head of all garden elves.

~ *Evelyn Foster* ~

The Garden had beds of bluebells, wildflower walks and mysterious hollow trees. It also had a small Magic House, which Elfrida had helped to build.

One day, in the run up to Christmas, Elfrida was in her garden when she got a message from Elwin. He always left messages for her under her secret squirrel statue.

Dear Elfrida (said the message)

Now you are one of us, could I send someone to see you?

He is High King Roland and he is having trouble with one of his leprechauns. No-one here in the magic realms seems able to help. So I thought picking the brains of an elf in the human world might do the trick!

Thank you.

From Elwin

~ *Garden of the Good Folk at Christmas* ~

Elfrida wrote back at once:

Elwin, I'd be glad to help but I'm not exactly an expert on leprechauns!

~ Evelyn Foster ~

Elwin soon replied:

I can easily give you some information:
Leprechauns are mischievous and love playing tricks: especially on humans. In fact, they are expert tricksters. They are extremely sharp-witted, and good at riddles and word games.

Leprechauns also love food and drink and they hold magic celebrations where there is dancing till dawn.

They are clever at imitating people too. They have learned, though, that is never a good idea to do an impression of someone if they are standing just outside the room!

May I send King Roland to you now?

From Elwin

Elfrida checked that nobody else was around, and then she replied to Elwin. That very afternoon, the Leprechaun King was standing in her garden!

~ CHAPTER TWO ~

THE KING OF THE LEPRECHAUNS

he Leprechaun King was small and stout. He wore a flowing green silk robe and a dashing tri-cornered hat.

"I am sorry to bother you, madam," said the Leprechaun King;

"but I do need your help."

"Of course, your Majesty." Elfrida smiled at him. "What can I do for you?"

The King looked rueful.

"It's not for me exactly. Gili, appear here, please!"

There came a flash of light. From it came an even smaller leprechaun wearing a green tunic, leather apron and red buckled shoes.

"This leprechaun," the King explained, "has been causing so much trouble that the leprechaun council want me to banish him from the kingdom!"

Elfrida's jaw dropped. She had not been expecting this. She knew that leprechauns were mischievous. But this one must have been bad indeed.

"Whatever has he done?" she cried.

King Roland gave a sigh.

"What hasn't he done?" he said, and he handed Elfrida a paper entitled:

WHAT GILI HAS DONE JUST THIS WEEK:
1. *Leading moth spirits into bogs so they end up neck-deep in mud.*
2. *Pulling rocks from under mermaids so they end up head-first in pools (which lost him his life-guarding job.)*
3. *Pouring orange juice over babies' heads at christenings so the babies get covered in orange.*
4. *Pouring water on sand sprites so they go wet and soggy.*
6. *Putting a spell on the shoes of princesses so that they can't stop dancing (which lost him his shoemaking job.)*

~ *Garden of the Good Folk at Christmas* ~

7. *Tying the wings of wind spirits together so they can't get off the ground.*

Elfrida gulped. Gili had certainly been busy! But surely there must have been a reason? She thought for a moment.

"Your Majesty," she said at last.

"Perhaps Gili has not yet found what he's meant to do in life? Maybe if I can find him a job he loves, his behaviour might well change?

"I hadn't thought of that!" said the King. He turned to Gili.

"That's settled then. Madam Elfrida will find you, let's see, two more jobs as you've been sacked from

two already! If you make a success of one of them, you can stay. But if you continue to be a nuisance, then you will be banished from the kingdom. This is your very last chance, Gili, I hope you realise that."

Gili gave him a big grin.

"It's a deal, then, King!" he said.

Elfrida's lips twitched. She couldn't help liking Gili.

"I will save him from banishment," she thought; "if it's the very last thing I do!"

Once the King and Gili had gone, Elfrida sat down in her Magic House to think. This was turning out to be quite a Christmas quest. How was she going to help Gili? That indeed was the question!

~ CHAPTER THREE ~

THE KINGDOM OF
THE LEPRECHAUNS

s leprechauns liked food, Elfrida decided she would try and find Gili a cooking job. First she wrote to Elwin:

Dear Elwin,

I'm trying to find Gili a cooking job. Can you help?

Love,

Elfrida.

It was not long before Elwin replied.

Dear Elfrida,

What a good idea!

If you pick an acorn from the oak tree in your garden, it will

take you to the Kitchens that serve the Leprechaun Cafes. I will arrange for Gili to meet you there.

The twisting of time in the magical worlds means that nobody will know you've been away.

From Elwin

Elfrida took a deep breath. She picked an acorn from the tree.

The garden started to shake. Then a pink cloud came and swept her away. Seconds later, to her delight, she was in the kingdom of the Leprechauns.

~ Garden of the Good Folk at Christmas ~

She found herself standing in an emerald valley. Although it was winter in the human world, in this magic realm, it was spring.

Above her, were four green hills each guarded by a castle. The trees were covered in green blossom and birds sang sweetly under a cloudless sky. In the distance, Elfrida could see a waterfall rushing over rocks.

In front of her were the Kitchens and a sign which said:

WELCOME TO THE KITCHENS IN THE LAND OF THE LEPRECHAUNS. PLEASE EAT AND DRINK HEARTILY.

Gili came to meet Elfrida and they went inside. The kitchens were full of steaming pots, boiling pans and leprechauns rushing about.

~ Evelyn Foster ~

Elfrida went up to the one who wore a badge saying: Head Chef.

"I've got a leprechaun here who needs a job," she told him.

The Head Chef looked very pleased to see them.

"We always need help, it's so busy here," he said, and he set Gili to work at once rolling pastry.

Elfrida felt pleased. It had been quite easy after all.

Before she said goodbye, she had a word with Gili: "Gili, I really hope you'll make a go of this," she told him.

"Remember it's your last but one chance."

Gili gave her a floury grin.

"It's a deal, Miss Elfrida!" he said.

~ Garden of the Good Folk at Christmas ~

When Elfrida got home, she wrote to Elwin and told him about the job she'd found for Gili. But would his new position work out? All she could do was wait... and hope!

That evening she found a note from Elwin under the secret squirrel statue.

Dear Elfrida,

Thanks for finding Gili that cooking job. It might well be the answer. Leprechauns certainly love to eat.

They also love gardens... though they do try to get out of the weeding!

A liking for country living is a definite advantage for a leprechaun.

Have a great weekend.

From Elwin

~ *Evelyn Foster* ~

Elfrida smiled and went to play with her friends next door.

They played Sleeping Beauty. Elfrida's best friend, Mimi, played Aurora as she liked sleeping in, and Elfrida played the Prince as she knew about roses. Mimi's little sister, Rhiannon, insisted on playing all the fairies, so she could use the play wand a Fairy Princess had once given her!

That night, when Mum and Dad were asleep, Elfrida flew to the Magic Kitchens. When she entered, she was met by chaos.

The vegetable chef was jumping up and down. The sous chef had water streaming from his eyes. The pastry chef had water streaming from his mouth.

"What happened?" Elfrida cried.

~ *Garden of the Good Folk at Christmas* ~

"This creature," said the Head Chef, seizing Gili by the scruff of the neck; "secretly put pepper in the fairy cakes and then made us all taste them. I want him out my kitchen now!"

Elfrida's heart sank to her boots.

~ CHAPTER FOUR ~

THE MAGICAL GARDENS

Elfrida took Gili out of the kitchens.

"Now, Gili," she said, sadly; "you only have one chance left. I'm going to get you a job at the Leprechaun Gardens. But you must behave yourself (and not try to get out of the weeding!) or you will be banished."

"All right, Miss," grinned Gili.

"Sorry about the kitchens but they were quite boring!" Wasting no more time, Elfrida took his hand and they flew over streets of shoemakers' shops to the beautiful Leprechaun Gardens.

Perfume rose from the flowerbeds, which were rich with red and green roses. Talking birds chattered in the trees, a lake sparkled over white

~ *Garden of the Good Folk at Christmas* ~

stones and the pathways were strewn with pearls. In the distance, they could hear happy shouts and laughs from a unicorn and pony riding school.

Elfrida went up to the leprechaun who wore a badge saying:

Oak: Head Gardener.

"I've got a leprechaun here who needs a job," she said.

Oak beamed. "As it happens, I need a fourth assistant gardener," he said. Elfrida thanked him and left Gili in his care.

~ *Garden of the Good Folk at Christmas* ~

Then she bit what was left of her nails and went home.

Could Gili escape banishment after all?

As soon as she got home, Elfrida wrote to Elwin to tell him the latest.

Almost at once she heard back:

Thanks for finding Gili the gardening job.

Leprechauns are often happier outdoors.

They tend to be found in magic burghs or hollow hills.

They hide their crocks of gold outdoors too.

So it's definitely worth a try!

Have a great evening.

From Elwin

~ *Evelyn Foster* ~

Elfrida smiled and fell into bed.

Next night, she flew to the Magic Gardens keeping her fingers firmly crossed.

Surely Gili would have stayed out of trouble this time.

Or, would he?

As she got to the gardens, Elfrida froze. Gili was putting a spell on the broom he'd been using to sweep leaves.

~ *Garden of the Good Folk at Christmas* ~

The broom chased the garden gnomes all round the Gardens.

It chased Oak to the edge of the Gardens where he fell in the compost heap.

It chased the second assistant gardener to the middle of the gardens where he fell in the lake. It chased the third assistant gardener into some stinging nettles where he fell flat on his face!

Oak had compost in his hair, the second assistant gardener had a fish up his nose and the third assistant gardener was covered in stings.

"I want that leprechaun out of my Gardens now," yelled Oak as soon as he could speak; "and I've messaged the King to tell him so!"

Elfrida felt sick to the soul. Now Gili would be banished.

She had tried so hard to help him. Yet it had all been for nothing!

~ *Evelyn Foster* ~

Elfrida was just giving way to despair, when a leprechaun from the riding school rushed in.

"The unicorns have got loose," he panted; "and they're galloping towards the waste wilderness!"

"Oh no!" cried the garden leprechauns. They knew what the waste wilderness was like. It was dark and full of monsters.

They all took care to keep away from it. Suddenly, Elfrida gasped. While everyone else had been panicking, Gili had jumped on a pony and was riding after the unicorns!

As she and the others watched, Gili spoke to the unicorns, very soothingly, until they all stopped running. Then Elfrida and the others rushed to join him.

"Well done, Gili!" Elfrida cried.

Gili turned his green gaze on her.

"I just love unicorns," he sighed.

Elfrida was about to speak when she saw

the other leprechauns bow. Elfrida spun round. Cantering up on a grey horse was the Leprechaun King. He drew himself up and glared at Gili.

"Time to banish you from my kingdom!" he roared.

~ CHAPTER FIVE ~

THE LEPRECHAUN KING

lfrida started forwards. "Your Majesty," she said. "May I say something?" and she told him what had just happened.

The King paused, and then turned to Gili. "What if I give you a job looking after *my* unicorns?" he asked.

Gili's mouth dropped open.

"That's an actual job?" he gasped.

"It certainly is," said King Roland; "and remind me to have a word with the leprechaun careers adviser. Gili, seeing as you saved these unicorns' lives, you deserve one final chance.

~ Garden of the Good Folk at Christmas ~

If I give you such a job, will you promise to stop behaving so badly?"

Gili smiled from ear to ear.

"All right, then King, I will," he said, and, amazingly, they all believed him!

A week later, Elfrida got an invitation from King Roland:

Dear Madam Elfrida,

We so appreciate you helping us with Gili, that we would like to give a party in your honour. Please will you and Elwin come to the Kingdom of the Leprechauns, to the heart of the Hollow Hills, next Friday at nine.

King Roland

So that Friday night, Elfrida put on her best dress and flew, this time with Elwin, to the Kingdom of the Leprechauns.

~ *Evelyn Foster* ~

The Hills were thick with buttercups and the leprechauns had filled them with glittering gold from their crocks. Leprechauns, elves, sprites, pixies and King Roland were all there.

Gili brought the unicorns to do a show for them. Elfrida and the others watched, spellbound, as the unicorns marched in the moonlight. It was a great party with plenty of food and drink, hill races, riddles and folk dancing. To everyone's astonishment, Gili was absolutely no trouble.

"And that," as Elwin said to Elfrida, "was the most amazing magic of all!"

~ *Garden of the Good Folk at Christmas* ~

~ CHAPTER SIX ~

THE CHRISTMAS HOLIDAYS

inter deepened in the human realm. The days grew crisper and colder.
The Christmas holidays arrived. The Magic Garden looked beautiful. Frost laced

the flowers and trees and gave the grass a walkway of white. Elfrida was just admiring it, when she got a message from Elwin:

Dear Elfrida,

Countess Glacia, head of the Frozen Kingdom of Polara, badly needs our help. Apparently she has a problem with a snow sprite and she needs a fairy godmother.

However, our usual fairy godmother, who handles this sort of thing, is away on holiday. I don't like to disturb her as she really needs a rest. Do you think you could stand in for her just this once?

Would you go to Polara and see what you can do?

I would be very grateful.

From Elwin

~ *Garden of the Good Folk at Christmas* ~

Dear Elwin (Elfrida replied)

I'd be glad to take this job, but I've never been anyone's fairy godmother before!

Don't worry, it's quite easy, Elwin wrote back:

Do you like to help people? Do you have a sympathy for those who are badly dressed? If you see people dressed in rags, do you have a burning desire to magic them up a balldress? If so, you are perfect fairy godmother material!

If you pick a snowdrop by the squirrel statue and twist it three times, it will take you to Polara.

Good luck!

From Elwin

Actually, thought Elfrida, she did like dressing up: herself, her dolls and sometimes other people. Perhaps she was right for the job.

Once she had checked that Mum and Dad were busy, Elfrida dressed warmly in her thickest coat and hat. Then she picked a snowdrop by the statue, twisted it three times and put it in her pocket. Soon she was flying to the magic kingdom of Polara!

~ Garden of the Good Folk at Christmas ~

~ CHAPTER SEVEN ~

THE KINGDOM OF ICE

lfrida had a lovely journey flying past snow-whitened trees and frozen waterfalls, past rooks, robins and reindeer. She flew over a tall man drawing patterns of frost on windows, and past a blue woman smiting the earth with a staff. At last, she reached Glacia's ice palace.

Two snow maidens in waiting, wearing warm robes and diamond veils, showed Elfrida into the throne room. Glinting icicles hung from the roof and sapphires encrusted the walls.

~ *Evelyn Foster* ~

As she entered, Countess Glacia rose to meet her: white dress flowing, her ice crown dancing with light.

"Elfrida, my dear!" she cried, joyfully.

"How very good to meet you!"

She helped Elfrida off with her coat and hat and they sat down to talk together.

"You said you had a problem with a snow sprite?" said Elfrida.

"Yes, indeed, "Countess Glacia replied.

"A new snow sprite, called Cristal, has recently come to live in our kingdom. We're a bit short-staffed on snow patterns at the moment so we were very glad to have her. However, Cristal hasn't settled at all. She is very shy and hasn't made any friends. I'm extremely concerned about her. All the winter sprites have tried to make friends with her. But if they knock at her door, she simply pelts them with fairy snow. We want to make her feel welcome, but we don't know what else to do!"

Elfrida thought for a moment. "Why don't you throw a big party?" she suggested at last. "Perhaps if Cristal can meet people without being singled out, she'll like it a whole lot better?"

Countess Glacia's eyes sparkled.

"That's an excellent idea!" she cried.

"I'm so glad you came, my dear. Now please excuse me, I have to see about a little boy called Kay. Apparently, he's been kidnapped by some awful Snow Queen."

Elfrida said goodbye and the magic snowdrop flew her home.

She felt very pleased she had been able to help.

When she got back, she wrote a message to Elwin.

~ Evelyn Foster ~

Dear Elwin,

I suggested if Cristal can meet people at a party, she might get on with them a whole lot better.

Love,

Elfrida.

This is good Fairy Godmother thinking (Elwin replied)

Fairy godmothers are always good at helping people: through both parties and christenings. If you are invited to any christenings, by the way, while being a fairy godmother, it is always advisable to give a present to the baby.

You, however, are clearly a natural fairy godmother.

From Elwin

Elfrida felt very proud!

~ *Garden of the Good Folk* ~

Yet the very next day, she had a troubling letter:

Dear Elfrida,

Please can you return to Polara as soon as possible?

Cristal has run away!

From Elwin

"Oh no!" cried Elfrida. She had to help Countess Glacia, she just had to. Elfrida wrapped up warmly again. She fetched the snowdrop and twisted it three times. Soon she was flying back to the magical icy kingdom.

~ CHAPTER EIGHT ~

THE WATERFALL

n Elfrida's arrival, snow started to fall. As she approached the palace, Countess Glacia hastened to meet her.

"Thank you so much for coming, my dear," she cried.

"Cristal is still a stranger to Polara and doesn't know its dangers. Will you help us look for her?"

"Of course!" Elfrida cried.

"Here is one of my chief sprites, Icenie," cried Glacia pointing to a sprite with curly blue hair.

"I'm sure she will be glad to help you."

So Elfrida and Icenie went to look through the mountains, while Glacia and her other sprites searched the ice plains and the snowfields.

They searched all through the mountains. But

there was no sign of Cristal. It was still snowing. Elfrida's hands were freezing, even in gloves. She could hardly feel the rest of her. But, doggedly, she kept on walking. They had to find Cristal. They just had to!

At least, the landscape was beautiful. They walked past shimmering icicles and gleaming blocks of ice. They walked past dazzling streams and shining masses of snow.

Next, they searched the frozen pine forests. But there was still no sign of the lost sprite. Elfrida was starting to lose heart.

Would they ever find her?

Finally, they hurried to the southern lakes: the only unfrozen part of Polara. Elfrida's heart skipped a beat. She had seen a tiny snow sprite in a lake. Then she went very still. The current was carrying the sprite towards a waterfall!

~ *Evelyn Foster* ~

It was clear Cristal had fallen in and had become too weak to fly or swim out. She could not escape and now she was in danger of falling over the waterfall!

"Cristal!" Elfrida cried.

Clearly, one of them had to get in the water. Elfrida looked at Icenie.

"I feel a bit of a headache coming on," said Icenie.

Elfrida gritted her teeth. It was up to her then.

Without further ado, she tore off her coat and shoes. She was just about to dive into the water when Icenie's hand shot out and held her back.

"Don't! It's much too dangerous," hissed Icenie. "You could drown or freeze to death. Not only that, it's too late – look!"

~ *Garden of the Good Folk at Christmas* ~

She pointed. Elfrida gasped in horror. Icenie was right.

Cristal was even closer to the waterfall. She was going to drop over the edge. Even if she was willing to risk her life, Elfrida would never reach her in time!

There was nothing Elfrida could do. She could not help it. She screamed.

Suddenly, as if by magic, Glacia and the other sprites appeared: alerted by Elfrida's scream. Because they could fly, they could reach Cristal quickly, easily and safely. Just as she was about to go over the edge, Glacia made a grab for Cristal's hand.

Then they all pulled her out of the water and onto the shore.

~ *Evelyn Foster* ~

Everyone sank, panting, down on the ground. Cristal was coughing, Elfrida, Glacia and the sprites were shaking.

Cristal gazed at all of them.

"So many of you," she whispered, when she could get her breath.

"I had no idea you cared."

"We certainly do," panted one of the chief sprites: "Why do you think we're all out here: dripping from head to toe!" She sneezed loudly and everyone laughed. Yet, looking at Cristal's face, Elfrida could see she now felt differently about her new home. Wet and tired as she was, she was glad to be in Polara at last. They had succeeded in making her feel welcome.

"And you," Cristal whispered to Elfrida. "You don't even know me and you were willing to risk your life for me. Just knowing I have a fairy godmother like you, makes me feel better about everything!"

~ *Garden of the Good Folk* ~

Despite the chill of the weather, Elfrida felt a warm glow.

She had been proud to be a fairy godmother to Cristal... even if just for a while.

~ CHAPTER NINE ~

THE ICE PAGEANT

he following day, back home, Elfrida got a secret message:

Dear Elfrida,

A thousand thanks for your help. Please come as my special guest to our winter pageant: Friday at eight thirty.

By the way, that little boy, Kay, is all right. He was finally rescued from that dreadful Snow Queen by a very brave friend called Gerda. What a relief all round, I must say!

Looking forward, very much, to seeing you.

Glacia

P.S. Icenie meant to write as well, but she thinks she's sprained her wrist.

~ *Garden of the Good Folk at Christmas* ~

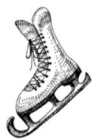

So on Friday night, when Mum and Dad were asleep, Elfrida flew to the winter pageant. There was ski jumping, snowboarding and fairy tobogganing. The ice sprites did an ice skating display followed by an ice hockey match.

The snow sprites, including a happy-looking Cristal, danced with snowflakes, while the frost sprites made delicate patterns in the air. Icenie did not join in, she was feeling a bit dizzy. Still at least her wrist felt better, and she cheerfully watched with the rest.

At intervals, they served the most delicious ice lollies, iced tea and countless flavours of icecream.

Elfrida found it hard to imagine what could ever top this.

"I wonder what the next excitement will be?" she

asked Glacia, rather wistfully, as they watched the ice dancing.

"I suppose it will be Fairytale Christmas," said Glacia.

Elfrida brightened at once. Christmas in the Lands of Fairy?

Now that would be something to celebrate!

~ CHAPTER TEN ~

A FAIRYTALE CHRISTMAS

Elfrida had goose bumps all over. It was nearly Christmas.

Already the house was full of mysterious smells and even more mysterious parcels. Only a week to go, yet Elfrida was not sure she could even wait that long!

She distracted herself by pruning her roses and tidying the borders: both useful garden jobs for this time of year.

Then, at the end of the week, she got a magic message from Elwin:

Dear Elfrida,

I wondered, as it is now the Christmas holidays, whether you might be free to come to Fairyland this Friday night?

~ *Evelyn Foster* ~

The Queen is ill and the King needs our help to organise Christmas (or Yuletide as they like to call it in Fairyland.)

From your friend,

Elwin

Elfrida's heart leapt for joy. They wanted her to help with Christmas in fairyland? She could not think of anything better!

Dear Elwin, (she wrote back right away)

I promise this will be the best celebration Fairyland has ever had.

Love,

Elfrida

Meet me in the gardens of Fairyland. (replied Elwin)

If you pick a four leaf clover and put it in your dressing gown pocket, it will take you there.

Sure enough, as soon as her parents were asleep

~ *Garden of the Good Folk at Christmas* ~

and Elfrida did as Elwin said, she found herself flying across the sea to Fairyland!

~ CHAPTER ELEVEN ~

FAIRYLAND

All the magic fairy islands lay across the western sea.

They appeared and disappeared in the blink of an eye, but Elfrida, having elf blood, could see them. She flew fast across the ocean: watching the flash of dolphins and the watery leap of the whales.

At last, she stood on the sands of Fairyland itself. Although it was night time, the moon shone so bright, the whole land was bathed in silver light. Elfrida found she no longer wore her dressing gown, but a beautiful satin dress.

The dress rippled and glittered whenever she moved. Luckily

~ *Garden of the Good Folk at Christmas* ~

the four leaf clover was still safe: in one silken pocket!

Elfrida stared at the headland above her. Tall trees shone in the moonlight. Their branches were heavy with strange purple fruit. Their leaves rustled softly although no wind blew. Built into a great green mound was a castle.

Elfrida left the beach and stood in front of it. It was a beautiful gold and crystal castle surrounded by a garden.

The garden was filled with giant flowers and softly singing fountains. The fountains sang strange songs Elfrida had never heard before. The garden paths were opal and shimmering plants grew leaves of rubies, sapphires and gold.

As Elfrida stood, marvelling, the door of the castle creaked open and Elwin appeared.

"Thank you for coming my friend," he said, warmly; taking Elfrida's hand and leading her into the Great Hall of the castle.

"We borrow the festival of Christmas from the human lands, but here in Fairyland it is special. The best event of all is the Yuletide Play. It's always performed by the Magic Theatre Company. I think they're doing Sleeping Beauty this year."

Elfrida's eyes shone. She loved plays and Sleeping Beauty was her favourite fairytale. This was going to be wonderful!

"You're welcome, Elwin; I really wanted to help," she told him.

Elfrida looked around the Great Hall. It had vast windows and a delicate painted ceiling. A huge lamp made from a single pearl hung from a silver chain. The walls were bright with crystals and gemstones.

"It's marvellous isn't it, Elwin?" she cried.

~ Garden of the Good Folk at Christmas ~

Before Elwin could reply, the King of Fairyland himself came to meet them. He was slim, stately and emerald-haired.

He looked noble, but rather stressed.

"I'm so relieved you're here," he said. "I just can't deal with Enchanted Yuletide on my own. The Queen usually does everything. She is so efficient. Can you two help me... please?"

"Of course, Sire!" cried Elfrida and the King nearly fainted with relief.

"Thank you, my lady!" he said, fervently; "this is what remains to be done." Handing Elfrida and Elwin a list, he turned round three times and disappeared.

Elfrida studied the list:

1. MAKE SURE WINTER SPRITES DECORATE THE LAND

2. ORGANISE YULETIDE TREE FOR THE CASTLE

3. CHECK ON PROGRESS OF THE YULETIDE PLAY

4. ARRANGE FOR LIGHTS TO BE UP ALL OVER THE LAND

5. ORGANISE YULETIDE FOOD

Elwin raised one eyebrow. "Do you think we can manage all that?" he asked, his lips twitching slightly.

"Definitely!" Elfrida replied. After all she had helped Mum organise her last birthday. This was bound to be easier.

Wasn't it?

Elfrida looked out the window that ran the length of the Great Hall. The frost fairies were painting patterns of frost, ice and snow on the trees.

"Well, at least that's one thing we don't have to worry about," said Elwin, following the line of her gaze.

"The frost fairies are already at work."

Nodding eagerly, Elfrida crossed number one off the list. Things were already looking good!

Some time later, the tree arrived. At first, the tree

~ *Garden of the Good Folk at Christmas* ~

fairies refused to leave the grounds and carry it into the Hall.

But after Elfrida spoke kindly to them, they did so. The tree was so tall, its top nearly touched the ceiling! It sparkled with silver frost. The fairies helped Elfrida put the tree in the centre of the room where it glistened in the glow from the candles.

"Perfect!" Elfrida cried and ticked number two off her list.

It was all going much better than she had expected.

Just then, two flower fairies rushed in. They were almost tripping over their tiny feet in their impatience to be first.

"Miss Elfrida," panted the first; "I want to be the fairy

on top of the tree. I'm by far the tallest!" and she studied her reflection in a mirror.

"Well..." Elfrida began.

"You! Who cares about you?" raged the other. "I'm the brightest and that's far more important," and she started to pull the first one's hair. In the corner, Elfrida could see Elwin stuffing a handkerchief into his mouth in a vain attempt not to laugh.

"Well," she said again; "excuse me? EXCUSE ME!"

To her relief, the two fairies stopped fighting and turned to her. Elfrida's mind worked quickly. There had to be a solution. There always was if you thought hard enough.

"Perhaps," she said, at last; "you two excellent volunteers could take it in turns to be the fairy on the tree? After all, you will both need some rest. Perhaps one of you could do it one day, the other the next and so on...?"

~ *Garden of the Good Folk at Christmas* ~

She held her breath waiting for the objections. To her amazement, they did not come.

"Erm, I suppose..." stammered the first fairy.

"I suppose that's actually quite sensible," sniffed the second, and to Elfrida's relief, they shook hands and agreed on it.

Elfrida worked out a timetable with them, and they both went away quite cheerfully.

"Well done, Elfrida." Elwin's eyes twinkled. "I think the King and Queen should take you on as a diplomat!"

Elfrida's confidence soared. If it was all going to be this simple, she did not need to worry.

Just as she was thinking that, everything went wrong!

~ Evelyn Foster ~

~ CHAPTER TWELVE ~

THE THEATRE OF MAGIC

"adam, Norris Nix, Director of the Theatre of Magic is here to see you," the King's butler announced, peering around the door.

"Please show him in," said Elfrida.

Norris Nix strode into the room. He was tall and dark with a flowing blue cloak.

"Welcome," Elwin greeted him. "What can we do for you?"

"Sir and Madam," said Norris. "I am sorry to inform you that there are many problems with the seasonal play, and, as usual, I am expected to fix it."

He sighed, theatrically, and continued.

~ *Garden of the Good Folk at Christmas* ~

"The fairy playing the Prince is allergic to the briar roses and has come out in spots. The Dawn spirit playing the wicked fairy refuses to wear black. The gnome playing the King has got his beard caught in the spinning wheel, and the pixies have spilt pixie dust over the backstage crew. They are supposed to be invisible. I've had enough. I am going on strike!"

"On strike!" cried Elfrida, aghast.

"But, why?"

"Because," said Norris; "although I have to put up with this sort of thing every year, nobody appreciates me."

"But everyone does appreciate you!" Elfrida began, sure she could deal with his objections as she had with the flower fairies. This would surely be another straightforward case. She just had to tell him what he needed to hear.

~ *Evelyn Foster* ~

"Hmm," sniffed Norris. "Well, nobody has ever said so to me. Until the kingdom shows me I am appreciated, there will be no Yuletide Play. Good night to you both."

Before anyone could speak again, he stormed out of the room!

Elfrida and Elwin looked at each other in dismay. There would be no Yuletide Play: the very best part of fairytale Christmas.

Elfrida was amazed that Norris did not feel he was appreciated. He was clearly a thoughtful and talented Nix.

Perhaps nobody had thought to actually tell him. They had just assumed that he knew.

Elfrida bit her lip. She had not handled it right after all. She should never have thought it would be easy.

~ *Garden of the Good Folk at Christmas* ~

Outside it was starting to grow light. Elwin patted Elfrida's hand.

"Try not to worry about it now," he said gently. "We'll come back and deal with it tomorrow."

Before they left, they went to see the Queen. The butler showed them into a grand chamber hung with silk and lace.

The beautiful Queen of the Fairies sat up in bed, her long hair falling over the covers. She took their hands in hers and looked at them, earnestly.

"Thank you so much for helping us," she said.

She looked so ill, they did not like to worry her about the play, and so they said nothing about it. They just asked after her health which was still fragile. Elfrida was very quiet as she and Elwin flew back.

~ *Evelyn Foster* ~

It was all very well Elwin telling her not to worry, thought Elfrida. She could not bear the thought of Fairyland having no special play. She had planned to help make the best ever Yuletide – and now it looked like being the worst! For the rest of that night, Elfrida could not sleep.

Next day, she helped Mum with human Christmas preparations: writing cards, addressing envelopes and hanging holly and tinsel round the rooms.

They went to the shops, and with the pocket money she had saved, Elfrida bought books for Mum and Dad. She bought a pocket

~ *Garden of the Good Folk at Christmas* ~

mirror for Mimi next door, as Mimi's little sister, Rhiannon, had accidentally broken her old one. She bought Rhiannon a tiny toy frog. Rhiannon really loved frogs and had once put one in Mimi's bed! She had probably expected it to turn into a Prince.

Elfrida wrapped all her presents. Then, next Friday night, she flew to the kingdom of Fairyland.

~ CHAPTER THIRTEEN ~

THE GOLDEN GLADE

On the way, Elfrida flew past sky elves polishing a sleigh. She saw star fairies putting fairy lights up throughout the kingdom, and knew she could cross number four off the list!

When she arrived at the castle, Elwin was already there with the cook. Elfrida greeted them both.

The cook served them both delicious rosehip tea and told Elfrida that Elwin had finalised the Yuletide food with her. So that was number five dealt with.

If only they could find a way to save the play, thought Elfrida, everything would be ideal.

But what could they do? She

~ *Garden of the Good Folk at Christmas* ~

had given the matter a great deal of thought. Yet she had not come up with anything and time was running out! Elfrida forced herself to stay calm and think again: letting her mind roam freely.

Then, suddenly, her face broke into a smile.

"I've got it," she cried, so loudly that Elwin spilled rosehip tea all over himself!

Elfrida ran to have a word with the King. Then, while Elwin mopped up his clothes and his tea, she rushed off to see Norris, Director of the Theatre of Magic.

Norris lived in a cottage in a golden glade in a forest of oak, ash and thorn. Norris was in his garden of magic talking plants. As

Elfrida rushed up, he was teaching them how to recite poetry:

"Up the fairy mountain, Down the rushy glen…"

"Norris," panted Elfrida as soon as she could get a word in; "the King would like to honour you and your group for your outstanding service to Fairyland. From now on, your grant will be increased, and your company will be known as the Royal National Theatre of Magic. You, yourself, will be known as Sir Norris of the Golden Glade."

~ Garden of the Good Folk at Christmas ~

The Director's eyes lit up.

"Thank you, Madam," he smiled; "my actors will be delighted. Oh, and in the circumstances I think we'll come back to work straight away!"

Filled with gladness, Elfrida hurried to report to Elwin.

Elwin seized her hands and swung her round in a dance.

"Congratulations, you're a genius!" he cried.

So, thanks to Elfrida, it was a marvellous Yuletide in the kingdom of Fairyland. The celebrations there were later than mortal Christmas so Elfrida could go to both. First, she had a glorious Christmas at home with Mum and Dad. They had cards and carols and presents and cake. Then they went next door and played charades with Mimi, Rhiannon and their parents. Elfrida went into the garden and told her robin friend all her adventures. Then she flew to the kingdom of Fairyland.

She and Elwin lined up with all the fairies. The Queen, who was now much better, gave them velvet clothes and jewels.

Lavish Yuletide cards arrived, delivered by fairyland robins. Elfrida gave Elwin a Christmas plant: a poinsettia, she had grown in her magic garden. Elwin gave Elfrida a gold acorn bracelet to match the ring he had once given her. That was Elfrida's favourite present of all!

They had a magical Yuletide dinner and then there was the play. Norris had solved all the problems. He had found the prince a hayfever

~ *Garden of the Good Folk at Christmas* ~

cure, rescued the gnome from the spinning wheel and trimmed his beard, persuaded Dawn to wear dark grey instead of black, and cleared up the pixie dust. The spinning wheel sang magical songs and the set was decorated with fireflies. It was truly enchanting.

After the curtain call, the King made a speech.

"Elfrida did have some serious problems in helping us," he said, gravely. Elfrida sat very still. Were they going to tell her she had done so badly she would not be welcome anymore?

The blood pounded in her ears. For a moment she could not hear anything. The King, however, was still speaking: "Yet, in spite of it all," the King continued; "not only did she manage to solve all these problems, she went on to give us the best Yuletide our kingdom has ever had."

~ Evelyn Foster ~

Suddenly, he grinned at her.

"Elfrida it was a good day for us when we asked you and Elwin for help."

Everyone agreed and cheered at the top of their voices. Elwin went bright red and Elfrida smiled so widely her face nearly split in half!

She flew home feeling happy, but thoughtful. She guessed there would be many other challenges ahead, but now she felt she could face them. What is more, she had absolutely loved being a Fairy Godmother – even for just a few days!

"And, now" called Elfrida, as she flew through the stars; "I'd like to wish everyone in all the worlds a truly magical Christmas!"

~ *Garden of the Good Folk at Christmas* ~

~ *Evelyn Foster* ~

~ Garden of the Good Folk at Christmas ~

~ CHAPTER FOURTEEN ~

ELFRIDA'S INSIDE GUIDE TO FAIRY GODMOTHERS

 o you think you might grow up to be a Fairy Godmother? Read Elfrida's inside guide and find out for sure!

A TENDENCY TO GO TO CHRISTENINGS

If you are invited to christenings a lot, you may become a fairy godmother. If you find that when a baby is born, you are top of the invitation list, fairy godmother blood may well be yours.

If you always get left off christening lists though, beware. This may mean you are a bad fairy!

Fairy Godmother Tip One: It is always thoughtful to give a present to the baby. Beauty, health and wealth are the most popular gifts. If you feel, however, you can't manage this, a china mug will do.

Fairy Godmother Tip Two: True fairy godmothers always say polite things about babies: even when the babies are sick on them. This is quite tricky, but true fairy godmothers can manage it.

AN ABILITY TO WORK SPELLS
If you find you can work spells: turn pumpkins into coaches, lizards into footmen and rats into coachmen, you are probably a fairy godmother. If however you cast spells over people, this simply means you are charming.

~ Garden of the Good Folk at Christmas ~

Fairy Godmother Note: It is worth remembering that fairy godmother spells often wear off around midnight. This can become awkward.

It is best reminding any girl you may be helping, to carry a spare set of shoes.

A TALENT FOR CHANGING INTO THINGS

As well as changing other people into things, a true fairy godmother can also change herself. Fairy godmothers can change into animals, birds and leaves as well as into other human types. So if you are good at pretending to be someone else, and if you enjoy dressing up, then the magic of fairy godmothers may be in you.

Fairy Godmother Tip One: It is sometimes a good idea to change into someone else if you get into trouble at home.

Fairy Godmother Tip Two: It is never a good idea to do an impression of people if they are standing just outside the room!

HAVING A MAGIC WAND

All fairy godmothers have a magic wand and learn how to use it.

Fairy godmothers need a wand to send deserving girls to balls, to produce glass slippers for them and to put fear into baddies.

So if you have a magic wand, or a play wand, you may grow up to be a fairy godmother.

Fairy Godmother Note: If you also have a magic costume, a crown and a pair of wings, then it is even more likely.

A KIND HEART

A Fairy Godmother is always kind. This means feeling sad when other people are in trouble and wishing to do something to help them.

Fairy Godmother Tip: It is always useful for fairy godmothers who are kind to have a box of tissues at hand.

HERBS, FLOWERS AND PLANTS

Real fairy godmothers know about herbs, plants and flowers and how they can be used in spells.

So if you are the sort of person who loves flowers: if you have your very own flower bed, herb garden or vegetable patch, then you may grow up to be a fairy godmother.

A LIKING FOR ROSES

As well as herbs and vegetables, most Fairy Godmothers have roses in their gardens. This is so that, if necessary, the roses can grow into a hedge that a prince has to fight through.

So if you or your parents grow a lot of roses this could mean you may become a Fairy Godmother.

Fairy Godmother Tip: When you are near any roses, be very careful of the thorns.

BEING A GOOD FRIEND

Fairy godmothers make very good friends. They know that the best friends are those who are thoughtful and loyal: not those who have the coolest belongings. Anyone who has a friend called Cinderella is almost bound to be a fairy godmother!

A Taste for Trendy Clothes

Fairy Godmothers have a good sense of style and like really interesting clothes. They like sparkly dresses, shimmering tights, glittery tiaras and shiny glass slippers. So if you have any of these in your wardrobe or dressing up box, you may have true Fairy Godmother blood in you.

Special note: You may alternatively grow up to be a rather original fashion designer.

A Sympathy for Badly Dressed People

On the subject of clothes, do you have a sympathy for badly-dressed people? If you see people in dull boring colours, or dressed in dirty rags and sitting by the fire, do you feel a desire to wave your wand and magic them a beautiful balldress? If so, you may well be or become a true fairy godmother.

A LOVE OF PINK, BLUE AND MAUVE

Although fairy godmothers are very fond of green dresses, they also love the colours pink, blue and mauve. These have long been popular shades for balldresses, and most self-respecting godmothers love them. So if you find yourself wearing clothes, painting or colouring pictures, or wearing jewellery in these shades, you may turn out to be a real fairy godmother.

~ *Garden of the Good Folk at Christmas* ~

Fairy Godmother Note: If you have a problem deciding between mauve, pink and blue when trying to dress a princess, you may be destined to work with Sleeping Beauty!

A LIKING FOR RATS, MICE AND LIZARDS

Anyone who likes rats, mice and lizards may well become a Fairy Godmother. If you like changing mice into horses, rats into coachmen and lizards into footmen you are almost bound to be one.

Fairy Godmother Note: Being able to turn pumpkins into coaches is an advantage for any fairy godmother.

AND NOW FOR THE FINAL TEST...

Go through your fairy godmother guide and think about all it has said.

Do you have a magic wand and crown? Do you like dressing up as a fairy at parties?

~ Evelyn Foster ~

If so, you may well become a Fairy Godmother one day.

Remember you don't have to tell anyone your secret – especially wicked wizards or witches.

Yet, if you do become a fairy godmother and are loyal and kind to all... you should live happily ever after!

~ CHAPTER FIFTEEN ~

ELFRIDA'S GUIDE TO MAGICAL LANDS

agical creatures have homes in all kinds of wonderful places. They live in forests, trees and flowers: in rivers, caves and streams. Some of them live in fairy lands which are all in hidden places.

There are believed to be magic lands beneath hills and mounds and on islands across the sea.

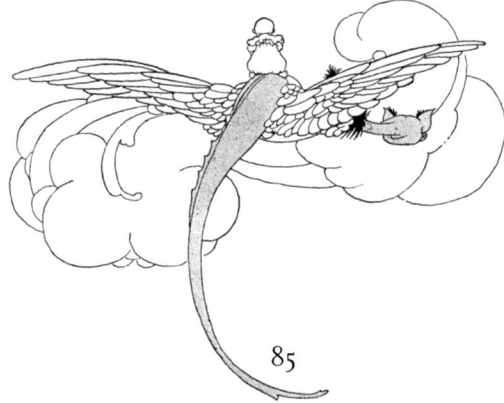

~ *Evelyn Foster* ~

Some enchanted islands disappear from sight as soon as ships appear! Here is a selection of some of Elfrida's favourite magic lands...

FAIRYLAND

Fairyland itself is a wonderful place covered in sparkling flowers. The shades in fairyland are stronger, the scents sweeter than those in the human world.

On a green hill stands the home of the Fairy King and Queen.

~ Garden of the Good Folk at Christmas ~

It is a beautiful gold and crystal castle surrounded by a garden. The garden is filled with fragrant flowers and sweetly singing fountains. It's paths are opal and it's shimmering plants grow rubies, sapphires and gold.

In fairyland, there are crystal rivers and sparkling silver seas.

The whole of Fairyland is bathed in a soft and shimmering light.

MAGIC UNDERGROUND KINGDOMS

Other magic kingdoms lie above or beneath the mortal world.

Many fairy creatures, for example, are believed to make their homes below hills or burghs with walls invisible to humans.

Their underground palaces are said to be beautiful: lit by the light of many glowworms. They have jewelled pillars supporting the roofs, walls covered with green and blue silk, magical paintings that move and speak, gold tables and flying chairs!

~ Evelyn Foster ~

MAGIC CAVE HOMES

It is thought beneath the earth there is a system of caves in which lies the kingdom of the dwarfs.

If you find the correct cave on earth and walk down a long passage, you will come to this underground kingdom. It has villages of tiny cottages and a turreted castle for its King.

Each of the village homes of the dwarfs gives off a glow like a miner's lamp. There are precious stones on the cottage walls and every home has marble floors.

~ *Garden of the Good Folk at Christmas* ~

AMAZING AERIAL KINGDOMS

Although most dwarfs live underground, one King has a home that hangs in the sky. It is set in an aerial garden of roses guarded by a magic silk thread. In the garden is a palace gleaming with the light of flaming torches. On summer nights, the people below drink in the perfume from the garden and praise the dwarf King, Laurin.

~ Evelyn Foster ~

Some fairies also have kingdoms in the air. They have lands of white-topped castles that humans mistake for clouds.

The floors are paved with gossamer and butterflies fly through the rooms. From their castles, the fairies look down on the mortal world below.

THE KINGDOM OF THE LEPRECHAUNS

The Kingdom of the Leprechauns is famous for its emerald hills, thick with buttercups, its bright green fields and valleys.

Waterfalls leap and rush over mossy green rocks.

The trees are covered in blossom and birds sing under a cloudless sky. There are individual houses and huts where the leprechauns make their shoes. There are many wonderful cafes and kitchens

~ *Garden of the Good Folk at Christmas* ~

where food and drink is served. In the middle of the country is a giant rainbow which, at its end, has a crock of gold!

MAGIC UNDERWATER LANDS

There are thought to be many fairytale homes beneath lakes, rivers and seas. Under the sea are kingdoms with castles made of shells and streets that are paved with pearls.

There are sea forests that glitter and glow and plants that never fade. Rocks are made of pure gold and sand is dust of silver.

Many of those who live in underwater lands drive chariots drawn by dolphins. They keep seahorses and cattle in great herds far beneath the waves.

Beneath the oceans there are thought to be sea caves of mermen and mermaids. Beneath the

Scottish waves, the Fin Folk, the Scottish water fairies, dwell. They inhabit a magic land where seaweed grows in every colour. The Fin Folks' favourite hobby is gardening, and their underwater homes are a medley of foliage and flowers.

Magical Lake Lands

Beneath the lakes of Switzerland, it is said, lies the kingdom of the Swiss water fairies. It is thought that whole towns lie beneath these lakes, with steep-roofed houses, winding streets and underwater parks. At evening, lights wink on in the houses and bells toll the hour.

The houses are white and surrounded by stones, and in their midst is a castle of glass.

Enchanted Forest Homes

Forests have always been preferred places for magical creatures to dwell. Fairy forests are vibrant with colour and contain the fairy trees:

~ *Garden of the Good Folk at Christmas* ~

oak, ash and thorn. Branches in fairytale forests overhang the path, and if you look closely, you can see eyes shining from the leaves! Lanterns hang from blades of grass and there are windows set in tree trunks.

All the plants and flowers can speak and are lit by tiny stars.

The main fairies who live in fairytale forests are the dryads (the tree fairies) and the daughters of the mountain gods who also like to make their homes in trees.

Dryads like to use heather and grasses for comfort in the homes, and they come out at night to feast and talk in groves. Many folk believe if you look carefully at trees, you can see the face of a dryad. Dryads make their homes in all sorts of

~ Evelyn Foster ~

trees, but their favourite is the willow. Willows which house a dryad are said to be able to pick up their roots and walk.

Dryad homes are tasteful: decorated with twigs, bracken and moss: with wooden tables and chairs.

If you creep into a fairytale forest at night, it is said, you can see dryads coming out of their homes and dancing in the light of the moon!

Within the root system of trees, moss maidens (the spirits who weave the forest moss) are also thought to dwell.

~ Garden of the Good Folk at Christmas ~

Beneath the roots of most forest trees, lies the hidden land of the moss maidens. They use tree roots as the canopy of their land and make their homes in the spaces below.

ELVEN HOMES

Elves, too, like to live in woodlands. They live in treehouses or have secret homes inside a tree. Other elves live in fine palaces in kingdoms which lie beneath fairy mounds. They have furniture of precious metals and chess sets made from gems. Elves carry bows and arrows tipped with flint to guard their lands from invasion.

THE KINGDOM OF ELFLAND

Some High Elves live in a special land of their own known as Elfland. This is a part of fairyland

...inhabited only by elves and ruled by a High King and Queen. Elfland is a land of spring, and is filled with plants which sway in a permanent breeze. Trees lean down and talk with fairies and roses play music from their leaves.

Elves chase each other through the woodlands and play with mice and fawns. Meanwhile, miniature dragons and unicorns run through the grass and flowers.

MAGIC FLOWER HOMES

Other fairytale homes are believed to lie inside flowers. Inside some flowers lie scented arbours and silken covered walkways.

~ Garden of the Good Folk at Christmas ~

This is where the pillywiggins or flower fairies live. They have satin furniture and sleep on beds of petals. It is thought that each flower has its own pillywiggin. Pillywiggins like to ride from home to home on the back of a bumblebee!

MAGIC MOUNTAIN HOMES

The great mountains of the world are also said to be home to magic creatures. The secret caves in mountains are thought to hide enchanted lairs.

There are many magical mountain kingdoms like Polara, where Glacia is the Queen, or Arendelle where Elsa and Anna dwell.

The caverns of the mountain kingdoms glimmer with frost. White mist rises from the rocky floors and water drops glisten like dew.

In Glacia's realm of ice and snow, there are shining icicles and gleaming blocks of ice. Alpine roses bloom beside the snowy paths. In Glacia's crown, there is a star-like jewel which dances with icy light.

CONCLUSION

Magic kingdoms exist in legend all over the globe. Fantastic beings are said to have homes in caves and mountains, beneath lakes and underneath the sea.

As long as mortals have had homes on the earth, there have also been fabulous magical homes in a secret parallel world!

~ ABOUT EVELYN ~

Evelyn Foster has worked as author, storyteller and actress. She has spoken on fairytales at the Royal Festival Hall and appeared in fantasy art as a dryad. She has read to the blind, performed in gardens and played an amazing amount of Fairy Godmothers!

She has run myth and drama workshops at the British Museum and judged writing competitions in care homes.

Evelyn has also written for newspapers, comics and magazines.

~ Evelyn Foster ~

~ OTHER BOOKS BY EVELYN ~

Include:

Garden of the Good Folk
The prequel to: Garden of The Good Folk at Christmas
(Country Books)

Frozen Fairytales for all Ages
(Country Books)

The Elves and the Trendy Shoes
(Tadpole Fairytale Twists)

The Mermaid Of Cafur
(Barefoot Books)

For much younger children:

Alan and the Animals
(Hachette Franklin Watts)

And for grown-ups:

Land of Hope and Story
(Country Books)